Barbie's®
ADVENTURES
TO READ ALOUD

By JEAN BETHELL

Illustrated by CLAUDINE NANKIVEL

WONDER BOOKS • NEW YORK

CONTENTS

BARBIE'S BIRTHDAY

Two more days! In only two more days it would be Barbie's birthday! Barbie sat down at her father's desk and looked at his calendar. Every day for the last two weeks she had looked at the calendar, counting the days till Saturday. Let's see—today was Thursday, tomorrow would be Friday . . . and on the very next day The Big Event would be here. What fun it was going to be!

Barbie loved birthdays—all birthdays—her mother's, her father's, her friends'. But, like all of us, her favorite birthday was her own. For Barbie, having a birthday was almost as exciting as Christmas.

Just think: one night when you go to bed you're five or ten or fifteen years old, a mere child. Then, like magic, when you wake up the next morning you're six or eleven or sixteen! Overnight you've become a grownup. You're not a baby any more. Of course, Barbie had noticed that when people become very ancient—when they reach twenty-two, for instance—they aren't as happy about having birthdays as they used to be. But she thought she understood why. After you've lived twenty-two whole years, you're probably very tired and feeble. But when you're still young, birthdays are simply wonderful.

"One of the nicest things about having a birthday," thought Barbie, as she put the calendar away, "is all the presents people give you. I wonder what I'll get this year? Right this minute all my friends may be out buying gifts for me. I wish I knew what they were buying."

But suddenly Barbie shook her head. This

was not a very nice way to act. Only greedy people think about receiving presents. She was behaving in a very selfish and self-centered way, and she must stop it this minute!

"I'm not going to think about my birthday even once more," she told herself firmly. "I'm not going to give it one single solitary thought until it's actually here."

Could she do it? She wasn't sure, but she was certainly going to try very hard.

Barbie managed to get through the rest of Thursday without thinking about her birthday, except for two mistakes. She made the first one at dinner time. Her mother served chocolate pudding for dessert, and the forbidden thought popped into Barbie's mind before she could stop it: "I wonder if she'll bake a nice big cake for my birthday?" Then later, at bedtime, she noticed how shabby her slippers looked, and quick as a wink a little voice inside her head whispered, "Maybe I'll get a new pair for my birthday!"

On Friday Barbie found it much more difficult to keep from thinking about her birthday. After all, tomorrow was IT. Tomorrow she would be a whole 365 days older than she was today. That seemed strange, but that was the way it would be. The whole idea was so interesting that Barbie really had to concentrate on *not* thinking about it.

Did you ever try to concentrate on not

thinking about something? Why not try it right now? Take elephants. For the next sixty seconds, see if you can keep from thinking about elephants. Don't let the word elephant, or the idea of an elephant get into your mind for a whole minute.

Ready? Go!

Oh-ho! Caught you! You thought about elephants, didn't you? Try as hard as you might, elephants sneaked into your brain and you couldn't keep them out. Well, that's the way it was on this particular Friday with Barbie and her birthday. The more she tried not to think about it, the more she *did* think about it! By the end of the day, her mind was almost dizzy from trying so hard.

She was very glad to go to bed and fall asleep that night. And luckily for her, the idea of a birthday didn't bother her once the whole night. Instead, for some reason, she found herself dreaming about elephants!

But the next morning it was different. Today *was* her birthday, and now she could think about it all she wanted to.

"Yippee!" she shouted, as she hopped out of bed. "I'm a grownup today! I'm a year older than I was yesterday!"

Suddenly she thought of something. Did she look a year older? Had her hair turned gray, or were there wrinkles on her face? She rushed to her mirror and looked closely at herself. What she saw made her feel much better. She was still a tall, slender girl with soft blond hair and a fresh young skin. There were a few wrinkles at the outer corners of her eyes, but she was sure those came from laughing, not from old age. Actually, she did not look a year older than she looked yesterday. But she did *feel* a bit more grown-up. Maybe even a bit more intelligent.

"Happy birthday, you grown-up, intelligent person!" she said laughingly to her reflection in the mirror. Then she got dressed, made her bed, tidied up her room and hurried downstairs to have breakfast with her mother and father. Would there be a present beside her plate? Would her father pretend to paddle her, one smack for each year? Would her mother serve something special to eat?

Eyes sparkling, she burst into the kitchen and stood for a moment waiting. But nothing happened. Her father was eating his cereal and reading the newspaper. Her mother was busy at the stove, breaking eggs into a frying pan. They had forgotten all about it!

"Good morning, Barbie," said Mr. Roberts, still looking at the newspaper.

"Want some scrambled eggs, dear?" asked her mother.

Barbie was amazed. Here it was, her birthday, and nobody had even mentioned it! It could have been any old ordinary Saturday morning. Well, *she* certainly wasn't going to bring it up! She'd never let them know how much they had hurt her feelings.

She sat down quietly at the table and drank her orange juice. By the time she got to her eggs, her father had finished the paper and seemed to be in a mood to talk. But did he talk about her birthday? No, indeed. He talked about almost everything else under the sun—the football team, the neighbors' dog, the weather. It was a pleasant conversation, and any other time Barbie would have enjoyed having her father talk to her as if she were a grownup. But today was different, somehow.

Maybe if she dropped a little hint, her parents would realize something was wrong. "My goodness!" she said, trying to sound casual. "Here it is the fifteenth of October again. It certainly doesn't seem like a year since the last time it was the fifteenth of October, does it?"

"No, it doesn't," said her mother calmly.

"Winter will be here before long," said her father.

"It's no use," Barbie told herself. "They've completely forgotten about my birthday. I might as well try to forget about it, too."

On Saturdays, Barbie usually spent the morning putting her clothes in order. Today she had to wash some sweaters and gloves and stockings. There were three blouses to be ironed. And several pairs of shoes to clean and polish. So after breakfast she put on her blue jeans and an old shirt and got busy with her work. When she had finished all her washing and ironing and shoe-polishing, she found still another job to be done. The hem of her favorite plaid skirt had become un-stitched, so she borrowed her mother's sewing box and began to sew the hem back in place.

As she worked, she noticed that the house seemed strangely quiet today. What was it? Then she realized that the telephone hadn't been ringing. On most Saturdays she received at least half a dozen phone calls from her friends and schoolmates. Ken Carson, the boy across the street, usually called to tease her about something. Her best friend, Midge, always called to discuss what the two of them were going to do over the weekend. But today, not a single call. She was deserted by everyone—her friends, her family. And on her BIRTHDAY, too!

Oh, well—no use moping around worrying about it. She finished hemming her skirt and sewed some loose buttons on her favorite green tweed coat. By then it was almost noon and she still hadn't heard from any of her friends. All right, if they wouldn't call *her*, she'd call *them*. She picked up the telephone and dialed Midge's number. Maybe the two of them could go to a movie or something. And maybe Midge would wish her Happy Birthday and cheer her up a little.

Midge answered the phone. "Hello?"

"Hi, Midge!" said Barbie. "What's new?"

"Hi! Who's this?"

"What do you mean, who's this? This is Barbie! Your friend, Barbie Roberts—remember?"

"Oh, hi, Barbie! I didn't recognize your voice."

Fine thing, thought Barbie. After ten thousand phone calls, she doesn't recognize my voice! What's the matter with everybody today?

"What's on your mind, Barbie?" asked Midge.

"Oh, nothing much. Just wondered if you'd like to come over to my house tonight, or go to a movie or something."

"Gosh, Barbie," said Midge, "I'd like to, but we're going to visit some friends this evening and I won't be able to make it."

"All right, Midge. Have a good time tonight." Barbie sighed and slowly hung up. Midge had forgotten her birthday, too. This was really turning out to be a terrible day. And it was going to be a long, dull evening, too.

Barbie spent the rest of the afternoon helping her father wash the car and doing little odds and ends around the house. It was nearly five o'clock when her mother called her into the kitchen.

"Barbie, would you run an errand for me?" she asked.

"Of course, Mom," Barbie said. "I need a little change of scenery, anyway."

Mrs. Roberts explained that she had forgotten to pick up the laundry this week, and wanted Barbie to do it for her.

"Your father needs a clean shirt to wear to his bridge club tonight," she explained.

While Barbie was changing from blue jeans into a turtleneck sweater and plaid skirt, she thought again about what she was going to do tonight. "Mother and Dad won't even be home," she groaned. "It's going to be awfully lonely around here. I'll get enough beauty sleep to last until my *next* birthday. Oh, dear, I shouldn't have thought of that word! Now I'm unhappy again."

As she started toward the laundry, Barbie looked at the Carson house across the street. But there was no sign of her friend, Ken. He's probably gone away, too, she thought. Why does everybody pick my birthday to go someplace else? She walked slowly down the street. No sense in hurrying. There was nothing to do when she got back, anyway.

After she picked up her father's shirts, she headed for home again. On the way she would pass the Sweet Shop. She decided to

treat herself to a big, gooey butterscotch sundae. Maybe that would make things seem a little brighter.

But when she got there, she saw a sign on the door reading CLOSED TODAY. Today of all days! It was a good thing her birthday came only once a year. She would hate to have to go through this misery any more often.

Slowly she strolled along, trying to think of something cheerful. She noticed the brightly colored chrysanthemums blooming everywhere. But their golden beauty could not lift her spirits as it usually did. She looked enviously at the smiling children playing on the lawns. She was glad *they* were happy, at least. It was getting dark as she finally walked up the flagstone path to the attractive white-and-blue house where she lived. The house seemed quiet. It even looked deserted, with no lights on, anywhere.

"I really am a Gloomy Gus today," thought Barbie. "I must snap out of it."

She walked up the front steps and across the porch. She opened the front door and went into the hall.

"Mother," she called, "I'm back with the laundry."

No answer. Where were her mother and father? Puzzled, Barbie started into the living room.

Then it happened!

"SURPRISE! SURPRISE!" The lights went on, and what seemed like a hundred people leaped out from behind the chairs and couches, shouting at the tops of their voices! Paper streamers flew through the air! Horns blew and cowbells clanked!

Barbie dropped the bundle of shirts and stepped back in amazement. What on *earth!*

Then in a flash she knew. It was a birthday party! A surprise birthday party! And all this time she thought she had been forgotten!

All her friends were there. They all wore paper hats, and Ken Carson stepped forward to put a blue derby on Barbie's head. Then Midge led the others in a loud chorus of "Happy Birthday, dear Barbie, to you." In the corner Barbie saw a table piled high with gaily wrapped gifts.

She could hardly believe her eyes or ears. This was the most *wonderful* surprise! This explained why everybody had acted so strangely all day—ignoring her and pretending they didn't know it was her birthday. This was why her mother had sent her to the laundry . . . so that all of the guests could arrive without her knowing it!

With a grin that stretched from one ear to the other, Barbie ran to her mother and father and gave them each a big hug. "Thank you *very* much!" she said.

Then, raising her voice so everyone in the room could hear, she said, "Thank you, *everyone*, for making this the best birthday I've ever had in my whole life!"

TRICK OR TREAT

SOMEONE was ringing the doorbell of the house where Barbie lived.

"Barbie, will you see who that is?" asked her mother. "I'm busy in the kitchen."

"Of course, Mother," Barbie said. She went into the front hall, switched on the porch light and opened the door. Then she stepped back in surprise. A ghost, a witch and a horrible monster were standing there!

"My goodness!" said Barbie. "What's going on here?"

"Trick or treat!" the visitors cried, flapping their arms and jumping up and down. "Trick or treat!"

It was Halloween, and all the boys and girls in the neighborhood were out. Each one was dressed in a fancy costume. There were ghosts and goblins, clowns and gypsies, pirates and cowboys, and even a couple of scary skeletons!

"Dear me," said Barbie, "I certainly don't want you to play any tricks! I guess I'll have to give you each a treat instead."

Of course, Barbie wasn't as surprised as she sounded. The little Halloween visitors had been expected, and Barbie and her mother were well prepared with candy corn, chewing gum, chocolate bars and lots of delicious cookies.

The ghost and the witch and the horrible monster each took a handful of goodies and dropped them into the big shopping bags they carried for just this purpose.

"Thank you!" they cried, and off they went

to collect some treats from the people in the house next door. Barbie smiled and waved good-by.

"I wonder how many other visitors we'll have tonight," she said to her mother. "I just hope we have enough candy and cookies to go around."

Then the doorbell rang again.

"Who will it be this time?" she said. "Clowns or pirates or gypsies?" But it was

23

none of those. It was Ken Carson, her friend and neighbor who lived across the street.

"Hi, Barbie!" he said. "Just thought you might need someone to protect you from all the goblins."

"I certainly do," laughed Barbie. "Come on in."

Ken hardly had time to take his coat off when someone pounded loudly on the door. It was four boys, all dressed as hoboes, with ragged clothes and dirty faces.

"Trick or treat!" they shouted. "Give us lots of candy or we'll rub soap on your windows!"

"I don't think that would be a very nice trick to play," said Barbie. "This is a night for having fun, not for being mean." She held out the big basket full of treats. The boys each took as much candy as they could hold in both hands, stuffed it into their bags, and turned away without even saying thank you.

"I wonder who those kids are," said Ken who was standing in the doorway with Barbie. "I don't think they live on this street."

"They're certainly not very polite," Barbie said. "I hope they don't play any harmful tricks on our neighbors."

One of Barbie's favorite neighbors was Miss Perkins, a sweet, white-haired little lady who lived alone in a very old house at the end of the block. Miss Perkins had been Barbie's teacher in second grade, and the two of them had been good friends ever since. Miss Perkins had no family, and she was quite lonely. Barbie often stopped in to chat with her. Sometimes Barbie's mother sent along some cake, or a basket of fruit or some homemade vegetable soup for Miss Perkins to eat.

Now, on Halloween night, Barbie thought about Miss Perkins, all alone in her old house. She hoped none of the masqueraders were bothering her.

Ken was still looking out the front door. The four hoboes had stopped in the shadow of some bushes at the end of the porch, and they were talking in low voices. Ken and Barbie listened carefully.

"Where shall we go next?" asked one of the boys.

"Might as well stop at every house on the block," said another. "The more stuff we get, the better."

"Let's turn over a few garbage cans along

the way," said the tallest boy, who seemed to be the leader of the group. "Might as well have some fun."

"We can soap all the car windows, too," suggested the short, fat hobo.

"And just wait till we get to old lady Perkins' house," chuckled the leader. "We can really have some fun there. We'll scare her good!"

Then the boys stuffed some candy and cookies in their mouths and walked across the Roberts' lawn to the house next door.

Barbie and Ken looked at each other in alarm.

"Poor Miss Perkins! We can't let those boys frighten her," said Barbie. "What shall we do?"

"Why don't we just take a walk down to the Perkins house and be there to greet the boys when they arrive?" Ken suggested.

"That's a good idea, Ken. I'll get my coat and tell Mother and Dad where we're going."

While the hoboes were collecting their Halloween treats from the people who lived next door, Ken and Barbie slipped out the side door, crossed the street and walked toward the Perkins house at the end of the block.

The lights were on in Miss Perkins' living room, and through the window they could see the little white-haired lady sitting in her rocking chair. Her head was tipped a little to one side, and she was fast asleep.

"It seems a shame to wake her up," Barbie whispered. "Let's just sit here on the front steps and wait for the hoboes to arrive."

Several groups of merry masqueraders went by, but none of them came up to ring the Perkins doorbell. All the neighborhood children knew that Miss Perkins was very poor and didn't have enough money to buy treats for everyone. Barbie and Ken smiled as they watched the happy children collecting candies from all the friendly neighbors along the street.

"They're having such a good time," said Barbie. "That's the way Halloween ought to be."

Then, from far down the street, they heard the rattle and crash of a garbage can being tipped over in somebody's driveway. The mean little hoboes were starting their tricks!

Soon they saw four dark shapes sneaking along the sidewalk. As the boys passed the house next to Miss Perkins' place, they pulled bits of soap from their pockets and rubbed them on the windows of a car parked at the curb.

"That does it!" said Ken. "I'm going to catch those little rascals."

"Wait a minute," said Barbie. "Let's see what they're going to do next."

The boys started up the sidewalk to Miss Perkins' house. "You dump over her garbage can," whispered the leader to one of the boys. "Joe, you rub soap on the windows. Mickey and I will swipe these chairs off the front porch."

At that moment, Barbie and Ken stepped out of the shadows into their path.

"Not so fast, there, boys!" said Ken sternly. "Where do you think you're going?"

The boys stopped short. "We're going to play Trick or Treat on the old lady who lives here," said the leader rudely.

"There's nothing wrong with that," muttered the short, fat boy.

"Of course not," said Barbie sweetly. "There's nothing wrong with playing Trick or Treat. We just want you to play it *our* way."

"What do you mean, 'your' way?" asked one of the hoboes.

"You boys are going to ring Miss Perkins' doorbell," Barbie told them. "And when she answers, you're going to say, 'Trick or treat.' "

The hobo laughed. "What's so special about that?"

"You're going to say it *very* politely," Barbie explained.

"Oh," said the boy.

"And then," Barbie continued, "when Miss Perkins says she'd prefer a treat to a trick, you boys are going to give her all your candy and cookies!"

"What?" the boys howled. "Why should we do that?"

"Because," said Ken, "if you don't, we'll tell your parents you've been dumping garbage cans and soaping windows."

"Don't do that!" cried the fat hobo. "My dad would wallop me!"

"I think all your parents would be very angry to find out what you've been doing," Barbie said. "Now, how about it? Will you play Trick or Treat *our* way?"

The boys looked at each other sheepishly. They knew Barbie and Ken meant what they said. "Okay, we'll do it," mumbled the leader.

"Go ahead, then," Ken urged. "We'll stand back here and make sure you do it right."

The boys went to the front door, and one of them rang the bell. Through the window

Barbie watched Miss Perkins. When the bell rang, she jumped a little, and her eyes flew wide open. A frightened look came over her face. She gathered her shawl around her shoulders, then slowly got up out of the chair and went to the door.

"Who is it?" she quavered, as she opened the door a bit and peered through the crack.

"It's Barbie and Ken and some Halloween masqueraders," said Barbie. "Go ahead, boys," she whispered.

"Trick or treat!" the boys shouted.

"Oh, dear! I'm afraid I don't have very much to give you for a treat," said Miss Perkins. "Would an apple be enough?" She sounded very upset.

Then Barbie spoke up. "Don't worry, Miss Perkins," she said kindly. "These boys are here to give *you* a treat. Isn't that right, boys?"

"That's right," they answered. "Happy Halloween, Miss Perkins!" And each one handed his shopping bag full of candies and cookies to the old lady.

"Well, for land sakes!" Miss Perkins exclaimed. "Isn't this nice? I never heard of such a thing!" She looked at all of the treats the boys had given her. "But this is too much for one person," she said. "I know! Why don't you all come inside? I'll make some hot cocoa for everybody and we'll have a nice little party."

So Barbie and Ken and the four hoboes

went into Miss Perkins' living room, where they spent a half hour drinking cocoa and enjoying delicious candy and cookies. When it was time to go, Miss Perkins asked the boys to take home all the things that were left over. "I could never eat it all," she said. The boys seemed very glad to fill their shopping bags again.

"Good night, boys," said Miss Perkins. "Thank you very much for giving an old lady a pleasant Halloween."

The tallest hobo smiled. "You're welcome, ma'am. We enjoyed it, too." He looked quite surprised at what he had said. Then the four boys raced out of the door, down the front steps, and headed for home as fast as they could go.

Barbie couldn't help laughing. "I guess that's the end of the Tricks and Treats for this year," she said. She and Ken rose to go.

"Speaking of tricks," said Miss Perkins, "I have an idea you played a little trick on those four boys tonight, Barbie. And I'm very grateful to you."

"So am I, Barbie," said Ken with a wink. "Considering all those good things we had to eat, it turned out to be a treat for all of us!"

THE LITTLE LOST DOG

"Look at that cute little dog," said Barbie. She and her friend Midge were just coming out the front door of Willow High School. A small gray poodle was sitting on the top step, near the door. He seemed to be waiting for someone.

"I wonder who he belongs to," said Midge.

It was Friday afternoon and the last class of the day was over. All of the students were hurrying home. As they streamed out of the door, the little gray dog looked anxiously at each face, but no one paid any attention to him.

Barbie bent down to pat him. "Hi, there, fellow!" she said. The fluffy gray tail waved back and forth in greeting. "I wish you were my dog," she said. "But I'm sure your owner will be along any minute now."

Then Barbie and Midge went on down the steps and started their long walk home. As they walked, they talked about many things —their favorite teacher, their homework, Barbie's new dress and their favorite television program.

They were only a few blocks from home when Midge happened to glance back.

"Look," she said. "We have company." The small gray poodle was trotting along behind them. As they walked, he came closer and closer, until he was following almost at their heels.

"I'd love to have a little dog like that," said Barbie, "but I can't."

"Why not?" Midge asked. "Don't your parents like dogs?"

"Oh, it's not that," Barbie explained. "They both love animals, but dogs make my father sneeze."

"That must be something like my Aunt Esther's rose fever," said Midge. "You should hear her sneeze whenever someone brings a rose into the room!"

By now the girls had reached the corner of the street where Midge lived. They stood there for a few minutes talking about their plans for the weekend. Then they said goodby. Midge turned to the left to go to her house, while Barbie crossed the street and turned to the right. "I wonder which way the dog will go," she thought.

She looked back. He stood on the corner, as if trying to make up his mind which girl to follow. He looked to the left where Midge was, then he looked to the right. Then, with a brisk wag of his tail, he turned right and hurried across the street to catch up with Barbie.

"He looks like a woolly gray lamb," Barbie thought. Then she remembered an old nursery rhyme: "Mary had a little lamb, its fleece

was white as snow. And everywhere that Mary went, the lamb was sure to go." Only this time it was *Barbie's* little lamb!

"I'm very sorry, little fellow," she told him, "but you'll have to stop following me. Why don't you go home now, where you belong?" But the poodle trotted right along beside her, head high and tail wagging. Barbie reached down and felt his neck. She thought he might be wearing a collar or a name tag. But he wasn't. There was no way to find out his name or where he lived. He was truly a little lost dog.

At last Barbie reached the white-and-blue house where she lived with her mother and father. "Good-by now, little friend," she said. "I wish I could bring you in with me, but I can't. Please go home now." She opened the door, and as she turned to close it behind her, she caught a glimpse of the dog sitting forlornly on the front walk, looking sadly in her direction.

Barbie went upstairs to her room. She changed from her school dress into a pair of slacks and a sweater. Maybe she could get some homework done before dinner. But instead, she found herself thinking about the dog. Maybe he's gone away by now, she thought. She peeked out of her window, and there he was, still sitting where she had left him. It would soon be dark. What would the poor little fellow do then? Who would give him his dinner? Where would he sleep?

She opened her history book and tried to concentrate on it. But the little gray dog kept popping into her mind. Before she went downstairs for dinner, she looked out the window again. He was still there. She felt so sad she could hardly eat a thing. How could she enjoy roast beef when just outside of the house a little dog was going hungry?

Barbie was tempted to tell her parents about the dog and ask if she could bring him inside. But she knew the answer would be no. She didn't blame them a bit, since having a dog in the house would make her father absolutely miserable. But she couldn't help feeling sorry for the poor lonely poodle. By the time dinner was over, she had made up her mind to do something about the little lost dog.

While her parents were in the living room, watching television, she put on a loose coat and slipped out the front door. The dog was

still there, shivering in the chilly night air.
Quickly she picked him up, tucked him inside her coat and carried him upstairs to her
room. She was quite sure her parents hadn't
seen him.

He was very happy to see her, and very glad to be inside a nice warm house. He trotted around the room, wagging his tail and sniffing at the rug, the chairs and everything he could find. Barbie found an old blanket and arranged it into a soft, cozy bed for him on the floor beside her own bed.

"Now you must promise to be very quiet," she told him. "If my father and mother find out you're here, you won't be allowed to stay. And please, for goodness sake, don't bark!" The dog licked her hand with his little pink tongue. Then he settled down quietly on his bed, as if he understood what she had told him.

Barbie walked back to the door. "I'm going downstairs for a while to look at television," she said. "Don't make a sound while I'm gone." The dog curled up into a small gray ball and closed his eyes as if to say, "I'll just take a nice nap to pass the time till you come back." Softly Barbie closed the door, and went down to the living room.

If Barbie's parents had any suspicions about the dog, surely they would say something to her now. But neither one of them mentioned the subject, and Barbie was able to relax and enjoy herself for the rest of the evening. First they watched a cowboy program; then a comedian came on and told jokes; and then they saw a story about ships. By then it was time to go to bed.

But first, Barbie went into the kitchen to get a little snack. Usually she fixed a sandwich for herself. But this time she wanted something for the dog. She cut several slices of meat from the roast they had enjoyed at dinner that night. She poured a large glass of milk. Then she said good-night to her mother and father and went upstairs with her food.

Barbie could tell that the dog hadn't been fed for a long time. He gobbled down the meat and lapped up every drop of the milk. Then he went back to his bed and settled down for a good night's sleep. Barbie was just ready to turn out her light and do the same, when she heard her mother and father coming upstairs.

"Quiet now, boy!" she whispered. "Not a sound."

She held her breath as her parents came down the hall toward her bedroom door.

Suddenly she jumped as she heard a loud "KERCHOO!" Her father was sneezing! He was standing right outside her door! Would he guess that she had a dog in her room? He sneezed again. Then once more. Fearfully, Barbie hugged the dog, expecting that any moment her father would open the door and look inside.

But luck was with her. "I must be catching cold," Mr. Roberts said in a surprised voice. Then he went on down the hall to the big bedroom. Barbie knew that she would have to send the dog away first thing tomorrow. It just wasn't fair to her father to keep him.

Barbie and the poodle were up bright and early on Saturday morning. While Mr. and Mrs. Roberts were busy in another part of the house, Barbie carried the dog downstairs in a large picnic basket and took him across the street to the home of her friend, Ken Carson. Ken and Barbie had known each other for a long time. They had gone to school together since the first grade. Each one always tried to help if the other had a problem. And today Barbie really had a problem.

She told Ken the story of how the poodle had followed her home, and how she had smuggled him into her room. She explained the strange effect dogs had on her father, and told him how unhappy she felt to hear him sneezing all night.

"Your poor Dad," said Ken. "I'll bet he's still wondering what made him sneeze."

"He's probably stopped, now that the dog is gone," Barbie said. "And now I just have to find another home for the poor little fellow. I don't suppose you'd like to have him? If he lived over here, I could come and see him every day."

"He's a nice dog, all right," said Ken. "But I don't think our two cats would be very happy to have him move in. I'm afraid we'll have to think of another solution to your problem, Barb."

"If only he could talk," Barbie sighed, as she patted the dog's head.

"By the way," Ken said. "What's his name?"

"I don't know," said Barbie. "I've just been calling him 'good boy' or 'little fellow' or 'hey you.' "

"Let's try a few dogs' names and see if he answers," Ken suggested. He led the dog a few feet away, and then he and Barbie took turns calling him.

"Here, Rover!" said Barbie. The dog just sat there and looked at her.

"Here, Prince!" called Ken. There was no reaction.

"Here, Curly! Here, Louie! Here, Wags!" they called. But none of the names made the dog perk up his ears or come running.

Suddenly Ken snapped his fingers. "I have an idea. Maybe his owner has put an ad in the paper for him. Have you looked at to-day's Lost and Found section?"

"Why, no," said Barbie. "I never even thought of that. Let's hurry and look."

Ken found a copy of that day's newspaper and turned eagerly to the Classified Ads on the next-to-last page. There was an ad saying someone had lost a diamond ring. Someone had lost a brief case full of important papers. A lady had found a striped cat. And there, way down at the bottom of the column, was an ad that said: "LOST: Champion white poodle named Pierre." The owner's telephone number was given.

"I guess we're out of luck," said Ken. "First of all, this little dog doesn't look much like a champion. Second, he's gray, not white. And third, his name isn't Pierre."

But Ken was wrong. At the mention of the name "Pierre," the dog jumped to his feet and ran over to Ken, wagging his tail.

"Here, Pierre!" said Barbie excitedly. The dog turned and ran to her side.

"Well, what do you know?" said Ken in amazement. "His name *is* Pierre! And maybe beneath all that dirt, he really is white!"

"Let's give him a bath and find out," said Barbie.

They took Pierre down to the basement

and put him into a tub half-filled with warm sudsy water. Pierre didn't seem to mind. He stood patiently while they washed him. They were careful not to get soap in his eyes. Once he tried licking the suds, but he didn't like the taste, so he didn't do it again.

Finally they rinsed him twice with warm water and dried him with a big beach towel. And sure enough, the little gray poodle was now a little *white* poodle!

"He *must* be the lost dog we read about in the paper," said Ken. "I'll go telephone the number in the ad."

While Ken was telephoning, Barbie put Pierre up on a table and brushed his coat till it was soft and silky. "You're a beautiful dog!" she told him. "I imagine you've won first prize at many dog shows." Pierre held up his right front paw, and they shook hands.

It wasn't long before a shiny black car pulled up in front of Ken's house. A man and woman got out of the car and started up the walk. Pierre was looking out of the window and saw them coming. He nearly went wild with excitement. He jumped up and down. He barked. He even did a couple of flip-flops. His people had found him at last! He was no longer a little lost dog!

Barbie and Ken smiled happily as they watched Pierre greet his owners. There was no doubt about it: he was definitely their dog. Between Pierre's barks and leaps, they introduced themselves and explained that Pierre had wandered away several days ago when someone left their back yard gate open. They had been terribly worried about him.

"I'd like to give you each a reward for finding Pierre and treating him so well," said

Mr. Wilkens, taking his wallet out of his pocket. But Barbie and Ken both shook their heads.

"Actually, it was Pierre who found *me*," said Barbie. "I enjoyed having him as my guest."

"Our reward is in knowing he has a good home to go to," Ken said.

Mr. Wilkens smiled. "My wife and I are both very grateful to you," he said. "We hope you'll come and visit Pierre often."

Barbie gave her fluffy friend a good-by hug. "You be a good boy," she said.

Pierre wagged his tail and licked her chin with his little pink tongue. Then Mrs. Wilkens fastened a bright red collar around his neck and carried him out to the shiny black car. He jumped up on the back seat and stood on his hind legs looking out the back window. As the car drove away, Barbie and Ken waved good-by.

Then Ken nudged Barbie. "Did you see what I saw?"

"Yes, but I don't believe it," said Barbie.

They both looked again, and it was true. Pierre had raised his paw and was waving right back at them!

THE SCHOOL PLAY

IT WAS almost three o'clock. In just a few minutes school would be over for the day. Barbie's English teacher, Mr. Sutton, had just finished today's lesson, and many of the students were closing their books, putting their papers away and getting ready for the final bell to ring.

Suddenly Mr. Sutton tapped on his desk with a ruler. "May I have your attention, please?" he said. "I have a special announcement to make. As you know, each year this class puts on a play in the High School auditorium. It's a very important event. All your friends and relatives are invited to attend. In fact, almost everyone in town comes to see it."

Barbie leaned forward so she could hear every word he was saying. The class play! How thrilling! Ever since she first started High School, she had been looking forward to this moment.

A boy across the aisle leaned over and whispered, "Now's your chance to be an actress, Barbie." A girl sitting three seats behind Barbie raised her hand. "When are you going to have tryouts, Mr. Sutton?" she asked excitedly.

Mr. Sutton smiled. "If you'll all stop whispering and talking, I'll tell you. All you budding young actors and actresses can try out for a part in the play, first thing tomorrow morning. We'll meet in the auditorium. Our play this year will be a modern version of an old-fashioned fairy tale. There will be a

Prince, a beautiful Princess, Knights in Armor, a Queen, Ladies-in-Waiting and a Dragon."

"A beautiful Princess," thought Barbie. "Oh, how I'd like to play that part!" But did she dare even hope? She knew there were several pretty girls in her class who would like to be the Princess, too. And many of them had acted in other plays, while she had never even set foot on a stage before.

Just then the bell rang and all the laughing, chattering boys and girls pushed their way down the aisles and out the door. Barbie stopped at her locker in the hall and put her books away, then went to meet her friend Midge under the clock in the front hall.

"My, but you look excited!" said Midge. "What happened? Did Mr. Sutton make a mistake and give you 100 on your English test?"

"Don't I wish!" Barbie laughed. "No, but it's almost as good. Mr. Sutton announced tryouts for the class play tomorrow, and I'm going to try for the part of the Princess!"

"Well, good luck!" said Midge. "I'd be scared silly to walk out on that stage in front of my parents, aunts and uncles and a thousand other people. I think I'll stick to painting scenery or selling tickets."

Enjoying the brisk autumn air, Barbie and Midge hurried down the street to meet the rest of their friends at the Sweet Shop. They settled down in a booth to enjoy their favorite after-school snack, butterscotch sundaes piled high with whipped cream. Everybody was talking about the school play. Three years ago a girl named Rosalind had played the leading part, and she had been so good in the part that a talent scout had offered her a part on a big television show.

"Gosh," thought Barbie as she ate her sundae, "maybe it will happen to me, too!"

She closed her eyes and imagined how it would be—her name up in lights above a Broadway theater, her picture in the papers and even on the front cover of a magazine, fame and fortune—

"Stop dripping!" said Midge sharply. "You're getting butterscotch all over the table!"

Barbie came back to earth with a jolt. "I'm sorry, Midge," she said, blushing. "I guess I was way up on a cloud somewhere."

Barbie could hardly wait to talk to her mother and father about the school play. That evening at dinner she told them all about it. "Do you think I have the slightest chance of getting the part of the Princess?" she asked her father.

"Of course I do, dear," said Mr. Roberts. "It's possible that you've inherited some acting talent from me. I never mentioned this, but when I went to High School, *I* was in the class play."

"Were you, really?" said Barbie delightedly. "Did you play the handsome hero?"

Barbie's mother laughed. "I'm afraid not, dear," she said. "I hate to say this, but your father played the part of a Christmas tree!"

With a very hurt expression on his face, Mr. Roberts went back to eating his lamb chops, while Barbie and her mother filled the air with laughter.

After the dinner dishes were washed and dried, Barbie went up to her room. She took along a big book of fairy tales her mother had read to her when she was a little girl. She was going to go about this acting business very scientifically and sensibly. First of all, she asked herself, how does a Princess look? She opened the book and found a picture of a beautiful Princess with long blond hair.

"Well, that's lucky," she said. "At least I do have long blond hair." She took off the clip that held her pony tail, and let her hair fall gently down over her shoulders.

Next, what does a Princess wear? The one in the book had on a long white dress and a golden crown. Barbie didn't have a long white dress, but she put on the next best thing—a long white nightgown. Naturally, she didn't have a golden crown, either. Perhaps a wide gold bracelet would do just as well.

Then she anxiously inspected herself in the mirror. Not too bad, she thought. With a real Princess costume and the proper make-up, she might look quite a bit like a real Princess. She just hoped Mr. Sutton would think so at the tryout tomorrow.

Barbie's next question was, how does a Princess walk? She moved her chair and lamp against the wall so that there was a large open space in the center of the bedroom. Then she practiced walking the way she thought a Princess should—slowly and smoothly, with shoulders back and head held high. She had to hold her head high, or the bracelet-crown would fall off. But at first she held it so high she couldn't see where she was going, and she kept tripping over the rug and running into the chair. But finally she learned the trick, and before long she was gliding back and forth quite gracefuly.

The last but most important problem was learning how to speak like a Princess. Barbie sat down in a chair and began to experiment.

"Ahem. Er—ah—oh, Prince Charming, where art thou?" she said in a soft romantic voice. Then, louder, "Hark! Methinks I hear the King approaching!"

Barbie couldn't help giggling. What would people think if they heard her talking like this? Still, a girl who wants to be an actress has to practice, doesn't she? All right, then, back to work. "Alas, the Duke of Devon has been slain by yon dragon! Oh, woe is me, the fates are so unkind!" Over and over, Barbie practiced speaking in her Princess voice.

It was quite late by the time she finished her rehearsal. But there were still two more things to be done before she was ready for bed. She had to pick out a dress to wear tomorrow. And she had to wash her hair so that it would be soft and shiny. After looking at all the dresses in her closet, she chose a pretty blue one with long sleeves and a full skirt. With it she would wear matching high-heeled shoes.

Then she washed her hair and carefully rolled it up on fat curlers. Finally, she went to bed and turned off the light. My, but she was tired! It wasn't easy, being a famous actress. Then she drifted off to sleep, dreaming that she was on the stage, taking bow after bow as the people in the audience clapped and cheered for the beautiful new star.

The next morning Barbie woke up feeling perfectly miserable! Her nose tickled. Her throat hurt. "Good morning," she said, and her voice sounded like a rusty door hinge. Oh, dear—she shouldn't have gone to bed with her hair wet. She shouldn't have opened the window so wide. How awful! Here it was, the Big Day—the day of the play tryouts—and she could hardly talk!

What should she do? Should she give up her dream of starring in the class play, or should she go ahead and try for it in spite of her sneezes and croaking voice? Perhaps Mr. Sutton would realize she had a cold. Perhaps he would give her the part because she could look like a Princess and walk like a Princess, even though she couldn't *talk* like one.

Barbie's mother was very sympathetic, and did all she could to cheer up her unhappy daughter. "You'll feel better after a good breakfast," she said, as she served Barbie her favorite jelly omelet and toasted muffins.

And she was right. Barbie did feel much better. The only trouble was, she still had red eyes, a sneezy nose and a hoarse voice. "Shall I call the whole thing off?" she asked her mother.

"Of course not, dear. Here are some cough drops that will help your throat. You just go right up there on the stage and show Mr. Sutton what a good actress you really are."

So Barbie put on her pretty blue dress with the matching high-heeled shoes, and hurried off to school. She had just taken a seat in the auditorium when Mr. Sutton walked out on the stage and said, "All you young ladies who would like to play the part of the Princess, please come up on the stage now."

Barbie and four other hopeful young actresses climbed the short flight of stairs at the side of the stage and sat down in a row of straight chairs. Then Mr. Sutton gave each girl a copy of the play with the lines of the Princess underlined in red pencil. "When I call your name," he said, "I want you to walk out to the front of the stage and read the speeches as much like a Princess as you possibly can. Speak clearly, but don't shout. And good luck to all of you."

A dark-haired girl named Lois went first. She had been in several school plays, and she was a very good actress. Barbie could see Mr. Sutton sitting in the front row of the auditorium, nodding his head in approval as Lois read the lines. "What a beautiful voice she has!" thought Barbie miserably. "Wait till Mr. Sutton hears my foghorn."

Marcia Nolan was next. She was a tall, slender girl with a graceful walk and lovely blue eyes. Barbie thought she was an even better actress than Lois. Her only drawback was her hair, which was flaming red and cut in a short, boyish bob. Not at all the way a Princess wears her hair, thought Barbie. But then she remembered that an actress can wear a wig, and the style of hair doesn't matter a bit. "I'll have to be very good to beat Marcia," Barbie told herself.

Two other girls got up and read their speeches, but Barbie was so nervous and so busy studying her own script that she didn't even hear what they said or notice how they looked. Suddenly she heard Mr. Sutton call her name. She cleared her throat nervously. She knocked on the wooden chair for luck, and stood up.

In the play, the Princess was supposed to be imprisoned in a tower. She hears the Prince coming on horseback. Running to the window, she leans out and says, "Prithee, kind sir, wouldst thou help a maiden in distress?"

Barbie ran gracefully toward the imaginary window. But she had taken only a few steps when she heard a grating noise and felt herself lurch to one side. She looked down and saw that the heel of her shoe had broken off! What to do? Bend down and pick up the broken heel? Turn around and run? Ignore it and keep going? That seemed to be the only thing she could do.

"Prithee, kind sir!" she screeched, and was so horrified to hear how terrible her voice sounded that she forgot all about her broken heel. Croaking wildly, Barbie wobbled to the tower window, leaned out—and dropped the script right on Mr. Sutton's head!

At first, only a few people had snickered at Barbie's plight. But now everybody in the auditorium was laughing, including Mr. Sutton who was holding his hand over his mouth, trying desperately to muffle the sound.

For a moment, Barbie stood there, stunned
—wishing she could drop through the floor
and disappear forever. But it was funny.
Even *she* had to admit that. And soon she
was laughing, too—laughing harder than

anybody. Back and forth she rocked, giggling and gasping, till tears were streaming down her face.

Finally Mr. Sutton managed to pull himself together and climbed up to the stage. "Thank you very much, everyone," he said, choking slightly as he struggled to keep a straight face. "You were all very good, and it's hard for me to know which one to choose."

"I know *one* person he won't choose," thought Barbie, as she sat down beside the other girls.

Mr. Sutton walked up and down. "All right, here's the decision," he said. "Betty and Jane will play the parts of the two servant girls."

"Well, at least I escaped that terrible fate," Barbie told herself with a sigh of relief.

"The part of the first Lady-in-Waiting will be played by Lois," said Mr. Sutton. The other girls clapped politely.

"And the part of the Princess," said Mr. Sutton. Barbie and Marcia looked at each other anxiously.

Mr. Sutton went on. "The part of the Princess goes to Marcia Nolan!"

Barbie gulped, put on a big smile and said,

"Wonderful! Congratulations, Marcia! I knew you'd get it!"

"Thanks, Barbie," said Marcia.

"Of course, you'll have to wear a long blond wig," Mr. Sutton told Marcia. "We can't have a Princess with a short red crew-cut!"

"Well, that's it," Barbie said to herself. "That's one dream that won't come true. Maybe I can help Midge paint scenery or sell tickets or something." She laid her script down on the table and turned to leave.

"Wait a minute, Barbie," said Mr. Sutton. "Don't go yet. I'm not quite finished."

Barbie limped back to her chair on her broken shoe and sat down again. What now?

"You know, you're quite a sight with that crooked walk and croaking voice," the teacher said. Barbie groaned. "Please don't think I'm making fun of you," he went on. "I'm serious. I'm going to give you a very important part." Barbie sat up a little straighter.

"I want you to play the part of the Wicked Old Queen," he said. Barbie nodded eagerly.

"And if you are as terrible on the night of the play as you were today," he went on, "I know you'll be the STAR of the show!"

A PRESENT FOR MOTHER

"I WONDER what's on television tonight," said Barbie's father as he settled back in his favorite chair.

Barbie turned to the TV page in the evening paper and looked at the programs scheduled for nine o'clock. "There's a program about traveling to the North Pole. There's a detective story we've already seen. There's a wrestling match. And then there's a show called Crazy Quiz."

Barbie's mother said, "Let's not watch the wrestling match, please."

Barbie's father said, "I don't feel much like traveling to the North Pole."

"Well, that leaves the Crazy Quiz," Barbie decided. She turned on the TV set and tuned it to the proper channel.

The Crazy Quizmaster was a chubby little man wearing a plaid jacket and a very large bow tie that moved up and down when he talked. The first group of questions was all about the different states in the United States.

"All ready?" asked the quizmaster. "What state is named after a President?" While the quiz-show contestants gave their answers, Barbie and her parents held their own private contest right in their own living room. They all answered the first question at the same time. "Washington!" they shouted.

"Next question: what state has the longest name?"

"Pennsylvania," said Mr. Roberts.

"I think it's New Hampshire," said Barbie.

"I think it's Mississippi," said her mother.

"The correct answer is North Carolina or

South Carolina," said the quizmaster. "They both have thirteen letters. Now I want you to tell me six states that contain girls' names."

"You go first, Barbie," her father said.

"Let me see. There's Virginia and West Virginia. And Georgia. That's all I can think of right now."

"How about Louisiana?" asked her father. "And Flori-da?"

"Very good!" said Mrs. Roberts. "The only one I know is Ida-ho."

"I have another one," said Barbie. "How about Minne-sota?"

"No fair," laughed Mr. Roberts.

For the next few minutes the program was interrupted for some commercials. First, a man in a bear costume appeared on the screen and tried to persuade everyone to buy a certain brand of tooth paste. Then three dancing dolls sang a song about a new kind of corn flakes. Then the quizmaster was back.

"The second part of our Crazy Quiz is all about holidays," he said merrily. "I want you to tell me what holiday comes in each month that I name. What holiday is in January?"

"New Year's," cried Barbie.

"How about February?" asked the quizmaster.

"I know—Lincoln's Birthday," said Mrs. Roberts. "Washington's Birthday, too."

"What holiday is in March?" the quizmaster asked. There was complete silence. Nobody in the Roberts living room could think of a holiday in March. But one of the TV contestants knew. "St. Patrick's Day!" shouted a lady in a big fluffy hat.

"You're right!" cried the quizmaster. "Now, who knows a holiday in April?"

"That's easy," said Barbie's father. "April Fool's Day."

"Easter, too," said Barbie.

"Is there a holiday in May?" the quizmaster inquired. Once again there was silence.

Then Mrs. Roberts said indignantly, "A fine family I have! Nobody even remembers Mother's Day!"

Barbie and her father looked guiltily at each other. "It's a good thing somebody reminded me," Barbie thought. "Mother's Day will be here next week and I want to give my mother something very nice this year."

After one more group of questions about movie stars, the Crazy Quiz was over, and Mr. Roberts turned off the television set.

"That's enough fun and games for tonight," he said. "Besides, it's getting near your bedtime, isn't it, Barbie?"

Barbie kissed her mother and father good night and went up to bed. But she didn't fall asleep right away. The television show had started her to thinking. What could she give her mother? She had a few dollars saved from her allowance, so money wasn't any problem. But she didn't want to give her mother just any old thing. Such a wonderful mother should have something special, something no other mother would receive. But how do you find something like that, she wondered.

You make it yourself, that's how! But what could she make? She would have liked to knit her mother a sweater, but there was not enough time left to do that. How about baking a big box of cookies, or a Mother's Day cake? No good. Her mother would be sure to find out what she was doing, and it would not be a surprise.

Finally she thought of something. She would paint a picture! Her mother had been looking for a picture to go on the wall above the couch. Barbie would do a nice flower painting that would be exactly what her mother wanted. She could paint it in her room at night and hide it in her closet in the daytime. Wouldn't Mother be surprised to find a beautiful new picture hanging on the wall next Sunday morning!

Barbie started on her project the very next evening. First she drew a picture of a vase with some flowers in it. But the vase was crooked, and the flowers looked like a bunch of lopsided lollipops. She decided it would be better to find a picture she could copy.

She sat down with a stack of old magazines and looked through them until she found a beautiful painting by a famous French artist. But copying someone else's picture wasn't as easy as she had thought. In her first copy, the flowers seemed too large for the vase. In her second copy, the vase was too big for the flowers. The third sketch was a little better, although the roses looked a bit like daisies, and the daisies resembled sweet peas. Oh, well, after she got the color on, nobody would know the difference, she hoped.

The next evening she started to color the drawing. First, the red roses. But she had trouble mixing the exact color she wanted. The red always turned out too orange or too purple. Finally, she mixed a lovely, rich rose shade that was just right, and she painted all the roses. The green leaves and stems came next. By now it was very late and Barbie had to put the painting and all the paints and brushes into the closet and hurry to bed.

On Wednesday evening she mixed up some bright yellow paint and began to color the daisies. The red roses she had painted last night were still wet and sticky, and she found it hard to color the daisies without smearing the roses. She was almost finished when her hand slipped, and ruined two of the roses. She had to spend the rest of the evening cleaning off the red smears and repainting the roses.

On Thursday evening Barbie filled in the blue cornflowers and the white lilies. Then she stood back and inspected her masterpiece.

It was terrible! It didn't look a bit like the painting she had tried to copy. She couldn't give this funny-looking thing to her mother!

But she had only two more days to think of something else. Mother's Day was next Sunday. The next afternoon, after school, she stopped at the hobby shop to see if she could find something pretty to make for her mother. First she looked in the jewelry department. There were lovely earrings you could make by gluing tiny, colorful sea shells together. There were bracelets to be made by twisting silver wire into circles and squares. Or you could string bright beads together and make a gay necklace.

Next Barbie came to the counter where they showed how to make things with yarn. You could knit sweaters, scarves or gloves.

And you could weave yarn into potholders, rugs or place mats for the table.

Barbie was thinking about making some place mats, but she changed her mind when she reached the next counter. Here you could buy pieces of leather to be cut into different shapes and made into wonderful things like slippers, wallets, belts and purses. There were many kinds of leather. Some leather was smooth and shiny, some was soft and furry. It came in many colors. This was something she would like to try. She would make her mother a beautiful leather purse with a design around the edge. That would be very much better than the picture she had tried to paint.

When the saleslady came, Barbie picked out a nice, smooth piece of honey-colored leather, and an attractive pattern for a purse. She also bought the small kit that held the tools she would need to work with the leather.

She wouldn't be able to start on the purse tonight, because she and Midge were going to a concert at the school. But tomorrow she would take the leather over to Midge's house, and stay there till she finished the job. She

was so excited—she knew her mother would really be pleased to receive such a fine gift.

By noon on Saturday, Barbie was hard at work on the purse. She had the leather, the pattern and the tools spread out on the desk in Midge's room. First, she laid the pattern carefully on the leather and traced around it with a pencil. Then, with the scissors, she carefully cut out the pieces. Using a special tool, she began to punch tiny round holes all around the edge of each piece of leather. When she finished that, she would fasten the pieces together by threading slender leather strips through the holes.

While Barbie worked, Midge was busy wrapping the gift she had bought for her mother. It was a fancy bottle of perfume. It was a nice present, all right, Barbie thought, but something you buy at a store is not as personal as something you make yourself. She was glad she had thought of this beautiful pocketbook she was making.

"How about taking time out for some milk and cookies?" Midge suggested. "We've been working pretty hard, and I think we deserve a rest."

"That's the best idea you've had all day," said Barbie. She laid aside the pieces of leather she was working on, and followed Midge down to the kitchen. They each had a big glass of cold milk and some warm, crisp cookies Midge's mother had just finished baking. Then, feeling refreshed, they headed back to Midge's room. But when they got there, a shocking sight greeted their eyes!

Midge's little brother, Albert, was sitting at the desk with the scissors in his hand, and he was cutting Barbie's leather into tiny pieces!

"Albert!" cried Midge. "You naughty boy!" She snatched the scissors from his hand, but it was too late. The damage had been done. The purse was ruined!

"Oh, Barbie!" Midge wailed. "I'm so sorry! I should have locked the door so he couldn't get in. Will you ever forgive me?"

Barbie looked sadly at the scraps of leather scattered all over the table. She swallowed hard, then forced a smile to her lips. "Don't be silly, Midge. It wasn't your fault. It was an accident."

Midge sent Albert downstairs to confess to his mother the terrible thing he had done.

Then she turned back to Barbie. "Of course I'll pay you for the ruined leather, but what will you give your mother tomorrow? It's too late to make another purse."

"Don't worry, Midge. I'll think of something." Barbie gave her friend a cheerful hug. "Don't look so gloomy. Everything will turn out all right."

But secretly, Barbie was wondering just

what she was going to do. She simply didn't want to buy her mother a last-minute gift. Somehow that wouldn't be right. She wanted her to have something special—something that would really show how much Barbie loved her.

As she walked slowly home, Barbie was busy thinking up ideas, but none of them were very good. Not until she was almost home did she finally hit upon the best idea of all. Better than the oil painting. Even better than the handmade leather purse!

That evening, Barbie could hardly wait to finish dinner and hurry upstairs to her room to get started on her new idea for a Mother's Day present. She sat at her desk and worked till almost midnight. Then she took a final look at her handiwork, gave a satisfied nod and climbed into bed.

The sun was shining brightly the next morning when Barbie awakened. "It's Mother's Day," she thought, "and I know it's going to be a good one."

Mrs. Roberts was in the kitchen preparing breakfast when Barbie came downstairs. Mr. Roberts was sitting at the dining room table. He had put a pretty little package at the place where Barbie's mother would sit. It was wrapped in blue paper and tied with a silver bow.

Barbie put a large white envelope beside the blue package. Mrs. Roberts came in with a tray of scrambled eggs, bacon and toast.

"My goodness, what's all this?" she asked as she saw the gifts on the table.

"Happy Mother's Day!" cried Barbie and her father at the same time.

"Well, aren't you nice?" said Mrs. Roberts. She put the tray on the table so they could all help themselves, and sat down in her own chair.

"Which one shall I open first?" she asked. "They both look very interesting."

She reached for the package and untied the silver bow. Carefully she unwrapped it and took out a white velvet box. Inside was a card that read, "To my wife on Mother's Day," and under the card there was a lovely pair of pearl earrings.

Mrs. Roberts held them up admiringly. "They're beautiful," she said, smiling fondly at her husband.

Barbie could hardly wait till her mother got to the next present. Would she like it?

What would she say? She tapped her fingers nervously on the table as her mother reached for the white envelope. On the outside, in very fancy red-and-gold letters, were the words, "To my favorite Mom." Mrs. Roberts read the words aloud, then opened the envelope and took out a card that also had some fancy printing on it. She read the card silently, to herself. Then she turned to Barbie and said delightedly, "Why, I think that's absolutely the nicest, most original Mother's Day present I've ever heard of!"

Thank goodness, thought Barbie. It *was* a good idea, after all!

"Well, what is it?" said Barbie's father curiously. "What does it say?"

Mrs. Roberts began to read aloud. "It says 'Happy Mother's Day. This card entitles you to twenty hours of Barbie's time, to be spent washing dishes, cleaning windows, ironing, or doing whatever jobs need to be done. From your loving daughter.'"

"That's wonderful!" said Mr. Roberts. He looked thoughtfully at Barbie for a minute. Then with a twinkle in his eye he said, "I think you should make another one exactly like it, and give it to me, for Father's Day!"

BARBIE'S BIG ADVENTURE

BARBIE had a job! It was the first job she had ever had, and she was enjoying the new experience very much. She was working as a leader at the summer camp in Willow Community Park. Every day she met with a group of younger girls for a class in nature study. She was teaching them about the flowers, the trees, the birds and many other interesting things that live in the world around us.

Barbie's friend and neighbor, Ken Carson, was also working at the summer camp. He gave swimming lessons at the beautiful new outdoor pool. He and Barbie usually rode their bikes to the park in the morning, and rode home together in the evening.

One day Barbie decided to take her group of girls on a hike. "Gather round, girls," she called, "while I tell you what we're going to do today."

"Is it something exciting?" asked little Janie.

"Are we going into the woods?" asked a girl named Martha.

"The answer to both questions is 'yes,'" said Barbie. "We are going into the woods, and it *is* going to be exciting."

The girls clapped their hands in glee. "Maybe we'll see a bear," said Betsy. "Maybe we'll see an elephant," said Ruth.

"My, my, such wild imaginations!" Barbie said. "There aren't any elephants in the woods, or any bears. But there are lots of birds and trees, and that's why we're going. We'll see how many different kinds of birds we can find, and how many different kinds of trees."

Barbie made sure each girl was wearing comfortable rubber-soled shoes. She told each one to take a light jacket or sweater along, in case it turned cool. Martha was put in charge of carrying a plastic bottle of fresh water. Ruth was to carry the sun-tan lotion. Janie carried a box of matches, in case they wanted to build a fire. The other three girls carried some sandwiches and candy bars for a mid-afternoon snack. Barbie had her pockets full, too: a book of bird pictures, and a book for identifying tree leaves. She also carried a small first-aid kit containing bandages, in case anyone fell and skinned a knee.

Barbie and her little troop passed by the swimming pool on their way to the woods. Ken Carson was busy teaching three small boys how to swim. When he saw Barbie, he called a short rest period, and climbed out of the pool to talk to her.

"Where are you girls off to?" he asked. Barbie explained that they were going on a nature hike. They would stop every now and then to study the trees and the birds. She told Ken they expected to be back in camp about four o'clock.

"Well, be careful, and don't get lost," Ken said. "Have a good time!"

He jumped back into the pool and continued the swimming lesson.

There was a wide trail leading into the woods, and Barbie led her girls that way. Soon the wide tracks began to narrow down until there was no trail at all. At this point, the girls gathered around in a circle, while Barbie showed them how to make a new trail of their own.

"About every ten feet we'll make a stone marker to show which way we came, and to guide us on our way back," she explained. "A small stone on top of a larger stone means 'straight ahead.' If you put a small stone to the right of a marker, it means 'turn right.' A small stone at the left of a marker means 'turn left.' "

Barbie asked Janie to gather some stones so they could practice making trail markers. When every girl in the group knew exactly how the three signals were made, Barbie stood up and said, "All right, let's go on with our hike."

Into the woods they marched in single file. "Isn't this exciting?" asked Janie.

"Yes," said Betsy. "I wonder where the bears are."

Every so often the group would stop and place a stone marker alongside their trail. The girls took turns gathering stones and forming the markers.

As they walked along, Barbie told them how to figure out which direction they were going.

"Who can tell me where the sun rises in the morning?"

"In the east," said Ann.

"That's right, Ann. And where does it set in the evening?"

"In the west," answered Ruth.

Barbie went on to explain: "Right now it's afternoon, and the sun is in the west. If we face the sun, we'll be facing west. If we face away from the sun, we'll be facing east. If the sun is on our left, we'll be going north. And if the sun is on our right, we know we're going south. Does everyone understand that?"

"I don't," said Janie.

"Neither do I," said Ruth.

Patiently, Barbie explained it again, but the girls still shook their heads in confusion.

"I have a hard enough time trying to make these trail markers face the right direction," said Martha. "I don't think I'll ever figure out which direction *I'm* facing."

"I guess it is pretty complicated," Barbie admitted. "Never mind. You girls concentrate on the trail markers and I'll keep track of the direction we're going. Right now the sun is at our left, which means we're walking north."

By this time they had gone a good distance in the woods, and the girls were getting a bit tired.

"Let's stop a while and rest," Barbie suggested. "We'll try to identify some trees while we're here." The girls spread their jackets on the ground, sat down on them and began to study the trees that grew around the clearing.

Meanwhile, back at camp, Ken Carson was busy teaching the boys how to swim. Most of them were doing very well, except for a pudgy little redhead named Harvey. Instead of learning to swim, he kept splashing the other boys and ducking under the water to pinch their toes.

"Harvey, that's enough nonsense!" said Ken sternly. "If you can't behave yourself, get out of the pool!"

Harvey stuck his tongue out at Ken.

"All right, out of the pool!" Ken ordered. "You sit up there in that chair and behave yourself. I'll appoint you lifeguard. Your job is to watch and make sure that everybody in the water is safe."

Reluctantly Harvey sat down in the chair at the edge of the pool. But he didn't intend to stay there for long. As soon as Ken turned his back, Harvey was going to slip away to the bathhouse and change into his regular clothes. Then he was going to take his knapsack and go rock-hunting. Harvey was a rock

collector. His hobby was finding rocks and stones of unusual shapes and colors. In his room at home he had several shelves filled with interesting rock specimens. Everywhere he went, he kept a sharp lookout for strange and colorful specimens to add to his collection. He was especially fond of one pink stone he had that was shaped like a star, and another one in the shape of a four-leaf clover.

Harvey waited patiently. Finally, Ken swam down to the far end of the pool to show the boys some swimming strokes. He had forgotten all about Harvey. Harvey saw his chance, and took it. He got up out of his chair and strolled casually to the bathhouse. Nobody missed him at all.

Barbie and her girls were all rested by now. They had picked out six different kinds of trees growing nearby. They picked a leaf from each tree to put in their nature book when they got back to camp. Now it was time to start hiking again.

"We'll walk for another half hour, then we'll stop for lunch," Barbie said. "Martha, will you put a trail marker here? Point it to the left, in the direction we're going."

Martha found three rocks. She put a small one on top of the big one, then put the third rock to the left of those two. Now they were ready to leave.

It was a beautiful summer day and the girls were really enjoying their hike. Along the way they saw many kinds of birds flying around or sitting on tree branches. There were robins, sparrows, cardinals and red-winged blackbirds. Once they thought they saw a bluebird, but it was flying so fast, it was hard to tell for sure.

After a while, they came to a beautiful little lake.

"Let's walk around the shore and see if there are any ducks or other water birds here," Barbie suggested. "I'll put a trail marker here to show that this is the place we turned to go around the lake. When we get back to this spot, it will be time to start home again."

Barbie found a large stone and put a small, round, white stone on top of it.

"Just to make sure we don't miss this marker when we come back, I'm going to put something on it to attract attention," Barbie said. "What can I use? I know, I'll tie my

blue hair ribbon around the top stone. We'll be sure to see that, on our way back."

And that's just what Barbie did. As they started around the lake, the girls looked back and saw the blue bow clearly up above the grass and weeds.

Halfway around the lake, the girls stopped to have something to eat. The lunch-carriers unpacked the sandwiches and chocolate bars. Martha, the water-carrier, gave everyone a drink of cool water.

While the girls were enjoying their lunch, Harvey, the rock collector, was heading toward the very same lake. He didn't follow the trail the girls had made, because he knew a short cut that would get him there much faster. He didn't even know the girls were there. He simply wanted to find some interesting rocks for his collection.

Harvey carried a canvas knapsack over his shoulder. Whenever he found a rock he wanted, he picked it up and dropped it in his knapsack. So far he had found only two good ones. One looked like it was made of green marble. The other was shaped something like a boxing glove.

Harvey wandered on until he was very

near the lake. Sometimes there were nice stones down by the water. Suddenly a flash of something blue caught his eye. What was it? Some kind of bird in the grass? Harvey hurried over to investigate. Well, what do you know? A round white stone all wrapped up in a pretty blue ribbon! The stone looked like an egg. He decided to take it for his collection.

Harvey picked up the stone, and leaving the bow tied around it, he tossed it into his knapsack. Then he headed back to camp. This time he walked along the trail the girls had made. Every now and then he saw two or three stones piled together. Not realizing that they were trail markers, he kicked at them as he went by. Soon there was nothing to mark the trail that Barbie and the girls had made.

After the girls had finished their lunch, Barbie looked at her watch. Three o'clock. The sun was getting lower in the west. If they were going to be back at camp by four, they had better get started. She helped the girls tidy up their picnic area, making sure they didn't leave any candy bar wrappers or crumpled paper cups behind.

"We'll all take turns scouting for the trail markers," she told the girls. "Betsy, you be the first one. You go ahead of us and look for the markers we left on our way in. As soon as you see one, call out and we'll follow you."

Feeling quite important, Betsy skipped on ahead of the rest of the girls. Soon she saw a familiar sight—a small rock on top of a larger one, at the base of a tree. That meant, "go straight ahead."

"This way, everybody!" Betsy called, and went on to look for the next marker.

After Betsy had found six markers, Barbie sent Ann ahead to be the scout. Everything was going along fine until Ann called back, "I can't find the next marker." Barbie hurried ahead to help Ann. But she was right, there was no marker in sight where the trail split into two parts! One trail led away from the lake, the other went on around it. Which way should they go?

Barbie tried to stay calm and think hard. If she remembered correctly, this was the place where they had first seen the lake. This was the place where she had put down a very special marker so they would be sure not to miss it—the stone with her own blue hair ribbon tied around it.

Surely a blue hair ribbon should not be hard to find. She sent the girls in pairs down each branch of the trail for a few yards. She didn't want them to go too far, as they could easily become frightened or confused and start to run. That way, they could easily get lost.

Barbie called the group back together again. Some of the little girls were beginning to look worried.

"Are we lost?" quavered Ruth.

"Of course not," said Barbie. "This is just a test to see what good hikers we are," she assured them.

"Now, girls, think hard," she went on. "Do you remember what I told you when we started today? The afternoon sun is in the west. If you walk with the sun on your left, you're going north. That's the way we walked when we came into the woods. Now, we want to go the opposite way. We want to go south, back to camp. Where will the sun be if we walk south?"

"On our right," said Martha.

"Very good," said Barbie. "So, you see, all we have to do is to take the trail that has the sun on the right side, and we'll be heading straight back to camp."

Secretly, Barbie wasn't half as confident as she sounded, but she didn't want the girls to worry. She smiled cheerfully. "We'll go this way, and be back at camp in no time at all!"

Harvey arrived back at camp just as Ken was finishing his last swimming lesson for the day. It was almost four o'clock, and camp would soon be closing. Harvey sat down on a bench and began inspecting the rocks he had found today.

By four o'clock Ken had changed from his bathing trunks to his regular clothes, and was getting ready to go home. As he looked at his watch, he remembered that he hadn't seen Barbie and her girls going by on their way back from the hike. They should be here by now. Maybe he had missed them when he was inside changing his clothes.

He asked Mr. Lewis, the Camp Director, if Barbie had brought her group back yet. Mr. Lewis said he hadn't seen them. He had also been wondering where they were.

"We'll give them a few more minutes," he said. "They're probably so busy looking for birds they forgot what time it was."

At 4:15 Mr. Lewis called Ken. "Still no sign of the girls," he said. "I think we'd better start looking for them. Do you have any idea where they were headed?"

"No, sir," said Ken. "Barbie didn't mention any special place. She just said they were going on a hike."

"Hmmmm," said Mr. Lewis. "They could be almost anyplace. The woods cover a very large area, you know."

"Yes, I do know," Ken answered. "And some of it can be quite dangerous. Our Boy Scout troop used to go on hikes there. I just hope the girls are all right."

As Ken and Mr. Lewis started into the woods to look for the girls, they passed the bench where Harvey was sitting and looking at his rock collection.

"Wait just a minute!" Ken said sharply, as he saw the rock with the blue hair ribbon tied around it.

"Harvey, what are you doing with that hair ribbon?" he asked, as he hurried over to the bench.

Harvey looked up guiltily and tried to stuff the stone back into his knapsack. "Nothin'," he said. "It's just part of my collection."

"Like fun it is!" said Ken. "I happen to remember that Barbie was wearing a blue bow just like that when she left on the hike today." He took a firm grip on Harvey's shoulder. "Come on, now, Harvey! Where did you get that ribbon?"

"Don't remember," Harvey muttered, looking down at his shoes.

"I think you'd *better* remember! And right this minute!"

"Okay, okay!" Harvey squeaked. "I remember. It was at the bottom of a tree, alongside a trail someplace."

"That's better," Ken admitted, "but not good enough." He explained Harvey's story to Mr. Lewis, and together they decided that Harvey ought to become a member of their search party.

"Now, Harvey, you're a smart boy," said Mr. Lewis. "I want you to lead us to the exact spot where you found this stone."

As Harvey was leading Ken and Mr. Lewis into the woods, Barbie was trying to lead her group *out* of the woods. If they were going in the right direction, they would come to the place where they had stopped to rest earlier that afternoon. If they were going in the wrong direction—well, she didn't want to think about that.

As they walked, she laughed and joked with the girls to keep their minds off their plight. For a while they sang songs. But gradually they grew quiet again, and Barbie could see by their solemn faces that they were becoming frightened.

For the first time in his life, Harvey was worried. He knew he had been wrong to pick up the stone with the hair ribbon on it. He had not meant to hurt anybody, but because of him, the girls were lost in the woods and Ken and Mr. Lewis were angry with him. If only he could remember *where* he had found the stone!

Then it came to him!

"I know! I know where it was!" he said excitedly. "At the fork in the trail right beside the lake."

"Good for you, Harvey!" said Ken, giving him a pat on the back. "Now, what's the quickest way to get there?"

Harvey showed him the short cut, and the three of them ran along the trail as fast as they could go.

It was at that exact moment that Barbie found what they had been looking for: a trail marker. And it was right where they had stopped before lunch to rest and study the trees. There it was—a small stone balanced on top of a larger one, with another stone pointing to the left.

Wonderful! They weren't lost any more! Even without the markers, she had managed to find the trail.

"How about another song, girls?" she said gaily. "And let's make it a happy one, because we'll be home in just a few more minutes!"

The search party was getting close to the lake when Ken stopped and held up his hand. "Quiet! Stand still a minute. I thought I heard someone singing!"

They listened carefully for a moment. He was right. Someone *was* singing! It sounded like a group of girls. And they were only a few yards away!

"Hooray! We've found them!" cried Ken. "Let's go!"

"Hold on a minute," Mr. Lewis said. "Let's not tell them how worried we were. Let's just pretend we ran into them accidentally." So they slowed down and began to saunter casually down the trail to where Barbie and the girls were.

"Well, hi, there!" said Ken, as he caught sight of Barbie. "Imagine running into you!"

Barbie whirled around at the familiar sound of Ken's voice. "My goodness!" she

said. "It certainly is nice to see you. Girls,
look who's here!"

Ruth ran to Mr. Lewis and started to cry.
"We were lost," she sobbed. "And I saw a
bear."

Mr. Lewis patted her head. "You weren't a
bit lost," he said. "You're on the trail back to

camp. Barbie wouldn't let you get lost. She's a wonderful leader." Barbie smiled gratefully at Mr. Lewis.

"It was *so* exciting!" said Janie. "We had a swell time."

"Well, now that we've found each other, let's get back to camp," Mr. Lewis suggested. "Come on, Harvey, you lead the way."

Harvey heaved a big sigh of relief and proudly marched along the trail. After all, Barbie had found her way back without the stone with the blue hair ribbon on it. Nobody was angry with him now.

Ken fell into step beside Barbie. "Was I ever glad to see you!" she said. "How did you ever find us?"

Ken held up the white stone with Barbie's blue ribbon on it. "Harvey picked this up and brought it back to camp. I recognized it and we came looking for you."

Barbie slipped the blue bow off the stone and held it tightly. "My good-luck charm," she said softly. Then she laughed.

"From now on, this will be my favorite hair ribbon."

"Mine, too," said Ken. And together they hurried back to camp.

A DAY AT THE BEACH

Barbie and Midge were sitting on the front porch, staring sadly into space. Neither one had said a word for a long, long time.

Finally Barbie sighed. "Hasn't it been a wonderful summer?"

"It certainly has," said Midge. Her sigh was even deeper and sadder than Barbie's. "It's hard to believe this is the last day of vacation."

The two girls stared off into space again. Barbie's mother stuck her head out of the door and looked at them. "My, but you look unhappy!" she said. "Is anything wrong?"

"School starts tomorrow, that's what's wrong," Barbie told her.

"But what's so terrible about that?" asked Mrs. Roberts. "You both like school, don't you?"

"Oh, school's all right, I guess," Midge said. "But it's going to take us a while to get used to it."

"We've had such a wonderful summer," Barbie explained. "Sleeping late every morning, loafing around all day."

"But Barbie," Mrs. Roberts interrupted, "don't forget that you spent a month working as a leader at summer camp."

"Yes, but the rest of the time we didn't do anything but relax and enjoy ourselves. Going back to school will be hard work."

"Just think," said Midge. "Walking that long distance every day in snow and rain. Fighting our way through the crowded halls. Walking up and down all those stairs. Doing exercises in the gym—"

"And worst of all," said Barbie, "walking home again every afternoon, weary and weak and loaded down with tons of books!"

"Barbie, stop!" cried Midge. "I get tired just listening to you!"

"Come on now, girls," laughed Mrs. Roberts. "It can't be *that* bad!"

"Well, maybe not," Barbie admitted. "But it *is* going to be a lot harder than being on vacation."

Mrs. Roberts asked the girls what they were planning to do on their last day of freedom. It didn't take them long to decide that question. They would go to the beach. They would lie on the sand and do absolutely nothing. They would rest and relax, and gather their strength for the terrible ordeal of going back to school. Mrs. Roberts agreed to drive them to the beach when they were ready, and pick them up later to bring them home.

The girls began to gather up all the things they would need for a quiet day at the beach. Bathing suits and caps, of course. Sun-tan lotion, sun glasses and wide-brimmed hats. Large beach towels to lie on, and smaller towels to dry themselves after swimming. Jackets, in case it got cool. A few books to read, and a portable radio. Some sandwiches and a thermos bottle of cold lemonade. And last but not least, a big, striped beach umbrella to shade them from the bright summer sun.

Finally, they were all ready. They each had

to make two trips to the car to carry all their equipment. "I thought this was going to be a lazy day," puffed Barbie, as she struggled to get the beach umbrella into the back of the station wagon. "I'm getting tired already."

When they arrived at the beach, Mrs. Roberts stopped the car near the picnic shelter, while they unloaded everything. "Have a nice restful time," she said. "I'll be back to get you at four o'clock." Then, with a cheery wave, she drove away.

The girls looked at the beach. It was crowded with people sunbathing, eating, swimming, wading, playing ball or just sleeping on the sand.

"We'll have to carry these things way up there around the bend where there's room to spread out," said Barbie.

Somehow they managed to pile everything onto each other's arms and shoulders, and went staggering along the beach until they found the perfect spot to set up camp: a nice smooth stretch of sand hidden from the crowd by a small sand dune.

"Thank goodness we found a place!" said Midge. "My arms are about to drop off from carrying all this stuff."

They put down their bags and bundles, opened the beach umbrella and stuck the shaft into the sand. They spread out the big towels. Then they took off their beach coats and flopped down on the warm sand.

Barbie opened the bottle of sun-tan lotion and rubbed some of it on Midge's back and shoulders. Midge did the same for Barbie.

The sun shone down brightly and a refreshing breeze blew in from the water. The waves came in and splashed gently on the sand. It was a beautiful day for resting. Barbie and Midge smiled lazily and closed their eyes.

But their eyes didn't stay closed for long. A huge rubber ball suddenly rolled down the hill and headed in their direction. Right behind it came a little girl, running as fast as she could to catch it.

"My ball, my ball!" she cried. "Stop it! Stop it!"

The ball rolled over Barbie's legs as she sat up in astonishment. It was followed by the little girl who narrowly missed stepping right on Midge's face.

Faster, faster went the ball, heading toward the water. The little girl couldn't keep up with it. Into the water it rolled. Then the waves began to carry it out from the shore.

The little girl watched helplessly and began to cry. Barbie looked at Midge, and Midge looked at Barbie. Then they both

jumped up and ran into the water to get the ball.

"Ooh!" Barbie gasped. "This water is ice cold!"

Midge's teeth began to chatter as they

waded deeper and deeper. But the ball was out too far by now. They would have to swim for it. In another moment the ball would be carried out to sea by a huge wave. But luckily, Midge and Barbie managed to catch hold of it just in time.

"Oh, thank you, thank you!" said the little girl when they gave the ball back to her. Clutching it with both arms, she carried it back up over the hill and disappeared from sight.

The sun was very warm, but Barbie and Midge were both shivering. Quickly they dried themselves with their towels. "Now that we've done our good deed for the day," said Midge, "maybe we can get some rest."

Still shivering, they stretched out on the sand again, closed their eyes and waited for the sun's rays to warm them.

They were almost asleep when suddenly a gust of wind sprang up, blew noisily down the beach and lifted their beach umbrella right out of the sand! It spun crazily along for several yards before coming to a stop. Barbie and Midge blinked in amazement, then raced after their umbrella. Another gust of wind caught their beach towels and blew them in the opposite direction. For several minutes they were very busy collecting all their belongings and putting everything in order again.

"I thought we came here to rest," said Barbie unhappily. "This time we'll put the umbrella so deep down in the sand that it *can't* blow out."

They scooped out a hole about two feet deep, set the pole of the umbrella in it, and then packed sand tightly around it. Now the umbrella was really firm.

Once more they shook the sand off their towels and settled down. "If this keeps up, we'll be too tired to go to school tomorrow," Midge complained.

"Surely nothing else can happen," said Barbie.

But she was mistaken. No sooner had they closed their eyes than a large, shaggy dog came bounding across the beach. Tail wagging and ears flopping, he skidded to a sudden stop, throwing sand all over the girls. Then he began to sniff. He had discovered the paper bag full of sandwiches! Before they could stop him, he picked the bag up between his teeth and scampered off with it.

"Stop, thief!" yelled Midge. She jumped to her feet and ran after the dog, but it was useless. He dodged the sun-bathers, zigzagged around the beach umbrellas, leaped over picnic baskets, and finally disappeared in the crowd. Midge was standing there gasping for breath when Barbie finally caught up with her.

"Well, there goes our lunch," she said. "Now we'll have to walk all the way down to the refreshment stand for something to eat."

Since Midge was still out of breath from chasing the dog, Barbie offered to go for some food. Midge went back to the umbrella to watch their things. When Barbie returned, after a very long walk, they ate their sandwiches hungrily and drank lots of cold lemonade.

"Thank goodness the dog didn't steal the thermos bottle!" Midge laughed. They were feeling much better now, but the food made them sleepy and they really felt the need for a nap. So they rubbed on some more sun-tan lotion, shook the sand off their beach towels and settled down. Maybe they could recover some of the energy they had lost chasing the beach ball, the umbrella and the dog.

It was so beautiful and quiet and peaceful!
The soothing splash of the waves lulled
them. From far away came the shouts of people at play and the faint sound of sea gulls
calling. Soon both girls were almost asleep.

BANG! POW! BANG! BANG! Barbie and
Midge sat up with a jolt. Six small boys

wearing cowboy hats ran helter-skelter through their camp, scattering bags and baskets every which way!

"Stampede!" screamed the head cowboy. Then he and his gang galloped over the sand dune and out of sight. They were gone as quickly as they had come. The girls blinked in amazement.

"What on earth was that?" asked Barbie.

Midge groaned. "Look at this mess! Nothing like a day at the beach for a little peace and quiet!"

Shaking their heads wearily, they straightened their things for the fifth time and sank back on the sand in despair. By now they were too nervous to sleep. They kept expecting something else to happen.

"I wouldn't be surprised if an airplane decided to land here," said Barbie. "Or if a whale swam in to take a sun-bath with us."

For a long time the girls sat there looking cautiously around to see what would happen next. But everything was quiet. No stray dogs, no noisy children, no runaway beach balls were in sight. Just a few birds flying lazily overhead and the soothing sound of the waves rolling in from the sea.

Now, perhaps they could relax. Barbie yawned and settled back on her towel. Midge burrowed a comfortable spot in the sand and covered her eyes with her beach hat. For three whole minutes everything was calm.

Then without any warning came a deafening clap of thunder! The skies seemed to open up and torrents of rain began to pour down on them! Not even their beach umbrella could keep them dry. In only a minute they were soaking wet.

"We can't stay out in this!" Barbie gasped. She began gathering up their towels and hats and radio and books and baskets and bags. Midge wrestled with the umbrella and finally managed to pull it out of the sand, close it and balance it over her shoulder. Then, battling the wind and the rain, they slowly made their way along the beach to the faraway picnic shelter.

But everyone else at the beach had the same idea, and the shelter was crowded with people trying to keep dry. Barbie and Midge found a tiny space in the corner, and stood there dripping and shivering.

"I give up," said Barbie.

"So do I," said Midge.

They looked at each other with their hair plastered down and water dripping off their noses. And they both began to laugh.

"You should see yourself," said Midge.

"Well, you wouldn't win any beauty contest yourself," Barbie chuckled.

Just then they heard a familiar and welcome sound. It was Barbie's mother, honking the horn of the station wagon. Joyfully the girls hurried outside to the car. By now the rain had stopped.

"Thank goodness you're here!" Barbie said, as they threw all their things into the back of the wagon. Wearily they climbed into the back seat.

"How was your day?" Mrs. Roberts asked cheerfully. "Did you get a lot of rest?"

"Rest?" the girls shrieked as they collapsed in sodden heaps. "We've never worked so hard in our lives! We hardly sat down the entire day!"

"That's a shame," said Mrs. Roberts.

They rode along in silence for a while. Then Barbie said firmly, "I'm glad this is the last day of vacation."

"Me too," said Midge. "I'm glad school starts tomorrow."

Mrs. Roberts was astounded. "Why, girls, what do you mean?"

"After what happened today," they said, "we think school will be a wonderful place to get some rest!"

Use this easy, convenient way to build your child's library of
Read-Aloud Books